REACH OUT...
...YOUR HAND...
WELCOME...
...TO THE LAND OF MAGIC!

...AND YOUR STORY WILL BEGIN!

Chapter 1 STRIVE FOR YOUR IDEAL PLACE

Contents

FWUMP
OW, OW, OW!
AGH! MY BROOM...
HEY!
AKKO CRASHED... AGAIN.
ARE YOU STILL SAYING YOU'RE GONNA BE A WITCH?
YOU CAN'T EVEN RIDE A BROOM.
WITCHES AREN'T COOL ANY-MORE.
GLARE
CACKLE
CACKLE
......
...I CAN BE ONE!
I'M GOING TO BE...
...A WITCH!
THROB
THROB

—WITCHES.
IN PICTURES AND OLD TALES, THESE WOMEN TEND TO BE...
...THE VILLAINS.

SOME-TIMES, THE POWER OF WITCHES HELPS PEOPLE.
AT OTHER TIMES, IT ENTER-TAINS THEM.
REPAIR
BUT THEY'RE NOT REALLY LIKE THAT.

JUST LIKE CHARIOT'S DID WHEN I SAW HER THAT DAY!
YUP!

EVEN NOW, THERE'S A MAGIC ACADEMY THAT CONTINUES TO PRODUCE WITCHES LIKE CHARIOT—
LUNA NOVA.

THAT'S THE SCHOOL I'M GOING TO.
FINALLY...
I'M FINALLY GOING...!
FROM TODAY ON, I...
BRIGHTONBURY STATION
TO THE PLACE WHERE CHARIOT STUDIED!
TO THAT HALLOWED GROUND!
...AM GOING TO BE A WITCH.

THIS!
INHALE
EXHALE
THIS IS THE AIR CHARIOT BREATHED ...!
EEEEE!
SNORT
OKAY!
SHUF
HELLO!
WHERE'S THE STOP FOR THE BUS TO LUNA NOVA?
I'M GOING THERE! JUST LIKE CHARIOT!
SNORT
SNORT
HUH ...?
I DON'T KNOW, BUT...
I EAN, THIS OWN ESN'T AVE—
THANK YOU!
BOW
I'LL ASK SOMEBODY ELSE!
WHIZ

HELLO!
DO YOU KNOW WHERE THE LUNA NOVA BUS STOP IS?
THE SCHOOL CHARIOT WENT TO!
WHERE'S THE BUS STOP!?
THE ONE THAT GOES TO LUNA NOVA...
BUS STOP ...
HMMM?
UM!
UM!
UM!
UM!

THAT'S WEIRD. HOW CAN THERE NOT BE A BUS STOP...?

IT SAYS THERE'S ONE ON THE MAP.
LEYLINE TERMINAL
BRIGHTONBU STATION

ACTU-ALLY...
HMM
...ISN'T THIS WAY TOO VAGUE?

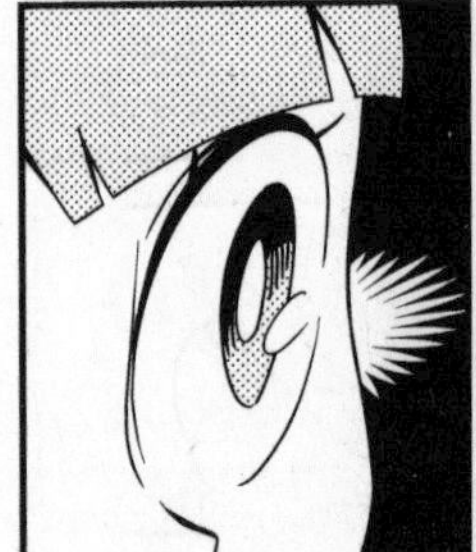

DASH
FOUND IT!
HFF!
HFF!
THAT HAS TO BE THE STOP!
TMP
THAT'S WHERE MY STORY WILL—
TMP
!?
WHUD

!

THIS IS—!

SHUF

PAT
PAT
!
BEAM

IS THIS YOURS!? ARE YOU A NEW LUNA NOVA STUDENT!!?
!
YOU'RE ON YOUR WAY TO THE ENTRANCE CEREMONY!?
ZOOM
OH, THANK GOODNESS!
...

TO BE HONEST, I WAS A BIT ANXIOUS ALL BY MYSELF.

I'M AKKO! I CAME FROM JAPAN!

HUH!?

STRIDE STRIDE

スタスタ

I SAW CHARIOT'S SHOW WHEN I WAS SIX...

...AND BEING A WITCH HAS BEEN MY DREAM EVER SINCE!

OR, WELL, NOT A DREAM.

DESTINY, MAYBE?

OF COURSE ...

...YOU DO KNOW HER, RIGHT? SHINY CHARIOT!

SEE!?

A RARE CHARIOT CARD!

FWIP

NOBODY BUT CHARIOT IS—

SQUISH

ZIP

BWEFF !!?

!
SHUF

SQUEAK SQUEAK
!?
!?

MMM!
TMP TMP
MM-MMPH!
JUMP

MM?

(WHOA, COOL! IS THIS MAGIC!?)
MMPH!
(MAGIC IN REAL LIFE! THAT'S A FIRST FOR ME!)

(...SOOO WHAT DO I DO ABOUT THIS!?)
WUAAAH!

SLIP

AGH ...!

KERSPLOOSH

SQUELCH

HFF

HFF

SLOSH

SLOSH

GEEZ. I'M SOAKED ...

THE SPELL CAME OFF, BUT...

HFF

HFF

~~~

~~~

OH!
THOSE ARE...
...LUNA NOVA UNI-FORMS!
DASH
DID YOU HEAR? THOSE TWO NEW STUDENTS COMING TODAY...
ONE OF THEM ISN'T FROM A WITCH FAMILY—
FOR REAL?
THEY'RE LETTING IN TOO MANY NORMIES LATELY!
THE SCHOOL'S IN FINANCIAL TROUBLE, AND IT CAN'T STAY AFLOAT UNLESS THEY LET EVERYONE IN, BUT STILL—
THEY'LL TARNISH THE PRESTIGE OF LUNA NOVA!
I BET SHE CAN'T EVEN RIDE A BROOM!
THADUMP
AS IF!

IN LUNA NOVA'S FIFTEEN HUNDRED YEARS OF HISTORY, THERE HASN'T BEEN A SINGLE STUDENT...

...WHO COULDN'T RIDE A BROOM.

YOU'D ACTUALLY GO DOWN IN THE HISTORY BOOKS FOR THAT.

...

AH-HA-HA! I DON'T WANT TO MAKE HISTORY LIKE THAT!

SNEAK

WHO'RE YOU?

FLINCH

A-AKKO... ...KAGARI...

I'M NEW.

!

AH HA HA HA HA HA!

?

?

WHOOP

THE LEYLINE TERMINAL ...
...IS A BROOM STOP!
!
THE LEYLINE IS LINKED TO LUNA NOVA.
MAGICAL ENERGY HAS BEEN RUNNING THROUGH IT SINCE ANCIENT TIMES.
IF YOU CATCH IT, YOU CAN FLY TO LUNA NOVA.
IT'S A MAGICAL HIGHWAY.
SWISH

LET'S HURRY.
ZWOOP
IF WE'RE LATE TO THE ENTRANCE CEREMONY...
...WE'LL BE EXILED FROM THE MAGIC REALM!
FLASH
......
WHAT AM I GONNA DOOO?

RUSTLE

LOOK AT YOU, CRASHING AGAIN!
YOU'VE GOT NO TALENT. JUST GIVE UP ALREADY.

I BET SHE CAN'T EVEN RIDE A BROOM!
NO WAAAY!

EVEN SO...
...I ......

HFF
HFF
RGH ...!
WHEN I REACH OUT MY HAND!
STRAIN
STRAIN
MY STORY!
STRAIN
WILL!
STRAIN
STRAIN
BEGIN!
GRAB
SNAP
HUH?

CLANK
CLONK
AWWW, GEEZ!
MOM AND GRANDMA GAVE ME TOO MUCH TO CARRY!
PHEW!
!
TOTTER
TOTTER
I'M GOING TO BE LATE —!

DID SOMEONE FORGET THIS?
I'LL HAVE TO GET IT TO ITS OWNER.
SHUFFLE
SHUFFLE
...
WHUNK
W-WILL THIS BE OKAY?
INHALE
O BROOM.
FLY...
FWOOSH
WHOOSH

TIA FREYRE!
FLOAT
OH GOOD ...
THIS SHOULD WO—
PHEW!
YEEK!!?
WHOMP
HUH!?
WHAT!?
WHO'RE YOU...!!?
TWITCH
TWITCH

ACK!
I- I'M SO SORRY! I DIDN'T MEAN TO—!!
HNNGH!?
I...
I JUST DON'T HAVE A BROOM ...

WELL, EVEN IF I DID, I DON'T KNOW HOW TO RIDE IT...
ARE YOU THE ONE THEY'RE TALKING ABOUT?

BUT I WANNA BE A WITCH ...
BWAAH!
...AND I WANNA GO TO LUNA NOVA...

I-IN THAT CASE, WANT TO COME WITH ME?
!
WE'RE SHORT ON TIME ANYWAY.

HUH? THESE ARE MY BAGS...
OH! A-ARE THEY?

THANK YOU!
GLOMP
SO THERE ARE NICE WITCHES TOO!
I'M ATSUKO! CALL ME AKKO!
I-I'M LOTTE. I'VE NEVER RIDDEN DOUBLE BEFORE, SO HOLD ON TIGHT.
OKAY!
OPEN!
PATH TO LUNA NOVA!
WE'RE FLYING!
HUH?
WHOA!
ZWOOP
FLASH
WHAT THE HECK IS THIS!?
VOOOOSH

GYA!
AAAH!
AAH!
EEEEK!
BAFF
I CAN'T! I CAN'T! I CAN'T! I CAN'T!
SCARY! I'M SCARED!
URP!
PLEASE CALM DOWN FOR A—
FOOOM

AAAAAAAAH!
OH NO ......
MY STUFF !!
TUMBLE
SOME-THING'S NOT...
!
IT'S NEVER BEEN LIKE THIS BEFORE...

LEY-LINES HATE SALT!!

HUH...?

HURRY!!

O-OKAY...

WAAAH

B-BUT WITHOUT PICKLED PLUMS, I'LL...

FWOOP

4/5
AGH!?
LUNGE
WAH!
MY TREA-SURE !!
WAAAH !!!
SCATTER

OOOOOO
THE LEG-ENDARY FOREST—
ARC-TURUS.
THE AVERAGE WITCH IS UNABLE TO ENTER IT... HM...?
FLIT
FLIT
KERSMACK
HUNH? WHAT'S THIS STUFFED ANIMAL?
SQUEEK!
WHUD
!?

VMMMM

FLUTTER
!
OW, OW, OW...

YESSS! MY TREASURE!
FWIP
I'LL NEVER LET YOU GO AGAIN!
PHEW!
GWUH!
HM?
"GWUH"?

CURSE YOU
FLINCH

EEP!
A DEAD—
RISE
THE PHRASE "PAIN IN THE BUTT"...

...WAS MADE FOR PEOPLE LIKE YOU.

OH!
KEH! KEH! KEH! KEH!
!
MEMORIES SURFACE

YOU'RE THAT...!
AAAAAH!

HM?

WE SEEM TO HAVE MADE IT TO MY DESTINATION...

!

DES-TINA-TION?

THEN THIS IS LUNA NOVA?

...THIS
FOREST
IS...
I WONDER
WHERE...

NO, IT
ISN'T.
I DON'T
KNOW
THESE
WOODS.

THE ARCTURUS FOREST...
POP

FWAP
FWAP

OH!
THE
FORBID-
DEN—

WHAAAAAT!!?
THE ARCTURUS FOREST—!?
WHERE'S THAT?

Little Witch Academia

Twinkle

Twinkle

Chapter 2 NOCTU ORFEI AUDE FRAETOR

THE ARCTURUS FOREST.

THEY SAY ONCE YOU WANDER INTO IT, EVEN WITCHES HAVE TROUBLE GETTING OUT...

THEN WE WON'T MAKE IT IN TIME FOR THE ENTRANCE CEREMONY!

NO WAY! WHAT A HASSLE!

IF YOU MOVE CARE-LESSLY—

!
SNAP
YEEEK!?
AKKO!
PFFT!
THIS WAY! HURRY!
SHOOM
WH-WH-WH-WHAT IS THAT!?
A MAN-DRAKE.
IT'S A MAN-EATING PLANT.

!

HUNH!?

FLING

LET ME BORROW THIS A SEC.

SNATCH

DRIP

HUH!?

!

HEY, WHAT DO YOU THINK YOU'RE—

FLAP

SQUAWK!

SQUAWK!

TWIST

IT'S PUPPET MAGIC!
OOOH!
WRITHE
WRITHE
WAIT, NO! WHAT ABOUT MY CHARIOT MERCH!?
WHAT ARE YOU DOING?
SHUF
SHUF
SHUF
THAT WILL DO.
?
HEY, ARE YOU LIS-TEN-ING TO ME!?
JURAS...
...HARAS ...HARAS...
PLIP
ROPE?
!
SWOOP
SHOOM

WHAT'S THIS?
RECITE THE SPELL.
THE SPELL?
HUH?
KAAA... FLALA.
OOOH...
SNAP

INHALE
KUTCHURA KATELA
FLALA!!
FLALA!!
FLALA!!
FLALA!!
FWOOOSH
!
THOOM
SILENCE
......
HFF!
HFF

THUD

THUD

"HEY, IDIOT. IF YOU DON'T LIKE IT, COME AND EAT ME."

FLINCH

D—

THUD

THUD

THUD

FLINCH

THOOM
BRAAAAWK!
DANG YOOOOOU!!

THAT'S IT. DRAW IT AWAY!
WATCH OUT FOR ITS PETRI-FYING BREATH.
SAY THAT SOON-ER!!!
DMM
DMM
DMM
DMM
DMM
FU FU!
SWISH
THE LEGENDARY COCKATRICE IS FOUND ONLY IN THE ARCTURUS FOREST.
THEY SAY ITS FEATHERS HOLD DEADLY POISON.
TOUCH
FOR A COLLECTOR OF LETHAL POISONS...
...THEY'RE AN ULTRA-RARE ITEM!!
SNAP
!
HEH HEH!
MINE!
OH. CRAP!
LOOM

I-I...
I... I...
DASH
DASH
DASH
DASH
DASH
...I CAN'T!
STOPPPPPP!
ooooo
...RGH!!!
CRASH
LOTTE!!
LUNGE
!

GRAB
A—
CRUMBLE

ARE YOU OKAY ...?
U-UH-HUH.

PULL
PULL
WE'VE GOT TO HURRY.
IF WE DRAG OUR FEET, WE'LL—

OW!!
FLINCH
!

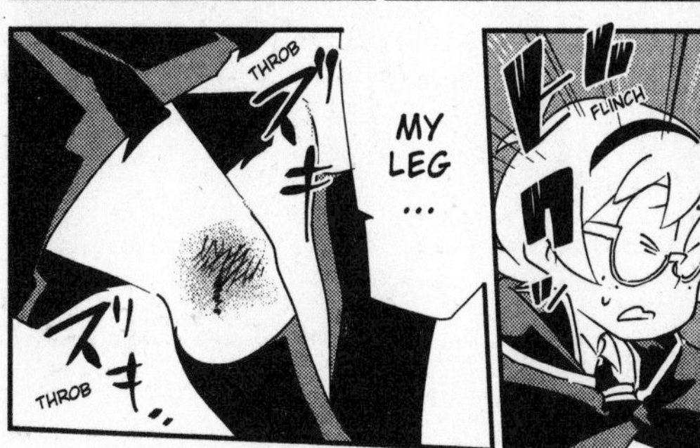
THROB
MY LEG ...
THROB

IT'S NO USE...
WE'LL NEVER MAKE IT IN TIME...

......!

PLIP

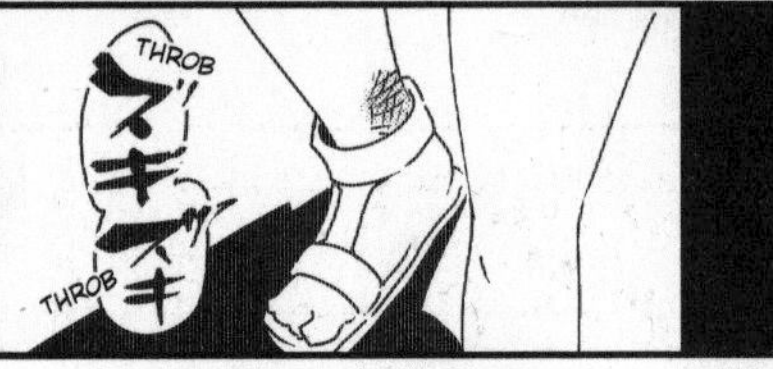

THROB
THROB

THAT'S NOT TRUE!
C'MON, WE'RE GOING!

I'M NEVER GIVING UP.
YANK!
NEVER!!

I'M GONNA ...
...BE A WITCH!
I JUST KNOW THAT WHEN I...
...REACH OUT MY HAND...
...MY STORY WILL BEGIN !!
HFF!
HFF!
!

ISN'T THAT...

...CHARIOT'S STAFF!?

WH- WHAT'LL WE DO? WE HAVE TO HELP HER, AKKO.
AAH...
......
LOTTE, YOU STAY HERE!
HUH?
TUG
RGH!
OOOO
HEYYY!
OVER HEEEERE!
!
KUT-CHURA KATELA FLALA!

DUMB OL' DOPEY-LOOKING CRITTER!
KUTCHUHURA
KAKATELA
FLALAAA!
BET YOU CAN'T CATCH ME!!
IRK
GRAAAAAAWK!
WHAP
HERE IT COMES!
!?
WHAT'S SHE DOING?
UMM!
AND NOW—
SQUAWK!

OVER THERE?
!
SCREECH
REAR
FINE ...!
OOOO
HERE GOES !!!
LEAP
WHOMP
SKIIID

OW, OW, OW!
POP

BRAWK?
FURL

GRAWK!
STRAIN
ギチ
!
STRAIN
ギチ

HISSSSS
DID IT WORK?
SQUEEK!
FLUMP
THANKS, ALCOR!
I OWE YOU ONE!

HEY.
NEED A LIFT?

THANKS...
TH—

...UM...
SQUEEK!
SUCY.
SUCY MANBA-VARAN.

THANKS, SUCY...
FWOOM
!?

GRAAAWK!!
GEEZ, IT'S STUBBORN!
WE CAN'T ESCAPE RIDING TRIPLE!
WHOOSH
FIIIIRE!!?
FWOOM
HOT!
ACH! THE BROOM'S ON FIRE!
PUT IT OUT!
WHIZ
FOUND THEM!

WHAT ARE THEY DOING IN A PLACE LIKE THIS!?
WHOOSH
THAT'S—!
!?
SHINY ROD!?
BLAST
GRAAAAH!!

FWOOM
!?
GASP
OH NO!
SAY THE "PHRASE" !!
AAAAAAAAAH!
AAAAH!
AAH ...
FLUTTER
!

RECITE THE SPELL!
WHEN I!
REACH OUT MY HAND!
MY STORY!
WILL BEGIN!
A BE-LIEVING HEART ...
...IS MY MAGIC !!

GRAB
NOCTU ORFEI...
NOCTU ...
ORFEI ...
AUDE!
AUDE!

FRAETOR!

FLASH
SHINYYY
ARC!!!

YYYYYY
ZING

SHOOM

VRRRM
GRAWK?
?
SHIIING

ALL RIGHT, THEN.

NOW...

...LET THE ENTRANCE CEREMO—

!

SHREEEEE
BOOMF
MURMUR
MURMUR
MURMUR
MURMUR
WHUMP
ZWIP
HUH?
FLUMP
OWW...

IS THIS...

...MAYBE...?

PUMP

WE MADE IIIIIT!

THAT ENTRANCE CEREMONY WAS UNPRECE-DENTED.

HONESTLY ...!

YOU WERE ADMITTED ONLY...
... BECAUSE THE PRINCIPAL GAVE YOU SPECIAL CONSIDER-ATION.
TAKE CARE YOU DON'T FORGET THAT.
BLAH BLAH BLAH BLAH BLAH
SQUISH
SQUISH
YES'M ...

THIS IS YOUR ROOM.
!
CREEEAK
GREET YOUR ROOM-MATES.

I'M AKKO!

LET'S ALL GET ALONG!

Little Witch Academia

Little Witch Academia

Chapter 3

AUGH, GEEZ!
IT'S SO BORING!!!
-UUUUUUGH!

WHAT'S WITH THE MYSTERY WRITING!?

I MEAN, COME ON!
SHOULDN'T MAGIC CLASSES BE MORE FUN!?
OH, AKKO... THIS AGAIN?

I HAVE NO IDEA WHAT SHE'S SAYING!
SNOOZE

IN THE WORLD OF WITCHES, CHARIOT IS A HERETIC.
CHARIOT TOOK CLASSES LIKE THIS!?
GWAAAARGH!
I CAN'T BELIEVE IT!
PIPE DOWN.
!
I CAN'T CONDONE HER MAGIC.
DIANA!
TEE HEE!
HEE HEE!
CLATTER
......

Chapter 3 THE WITCH FROM THE EAST

HEY! WHAT DO YOU MEAN!?
A-AKKO ...!
BLOW
ABOUT WHAT?

BAM
CHARIOT'S MAGIC ISN'T WRONG.
!

TAKE IT BACK!

NO.
I SHAN'T.
HNRGH!
EVEN IF CHARIOT WAS CORRECT ...
CLINK
...YOUR ATTITUDE IN CLASS WOULD RUIN IT.
REFLECT ON YOUR CONDUCT.
GHK!
SPLUT
SHE JUST GOT OWNED.
!!
VWIP
SUCY.
HEH HEH!
IT WAS TOO PERFECT. I HAD TO.
RGH!
SHE'S RIGHT.
YOU'VE GOT SOME NERVE.

ALL THIS WHEN YOU CAN'T EVEN RIDE A BROOM.
URRRR!
MAYBE CHARIOT COULDN'T RIDE ONE EITHER?

WHY, YOOOOU!
GIRLS, GIRLS.
VWIP
WHATEVER'S THE MATTER?
FLINCH
!

CALM DOWN, MISS KAGARI.
URRR...
BUUUT ...
MISS KAGARI IS NEW HERE, AND SHE ISN'T USED TO US YET.
UH-HUH...

OH!
I KNOW! MY NEXT CLASS IS RECREATION.
Nice idea!
IN ORDER TO DEEPEN FRIEND-SHIPS—

LET'S PLAY BALL!

HUH?

FLAP
...
WHY A BALL GAME?
THIS IS ALL YOUR FAULT.
NOW, NOW.
LOTTE! SUCY! ARE YOU...?
...ON YOUR TEAM. YES.
I WONDER WHAT WE'LL BE PLAYING.
THEY SAID VOLLEY-BALL.
I'M BAD AT THAT ONE...
YEESH. YOU PEOPLE?
!

WHAT A DRAG...
THAT'S IT. WE'RE GONNA LOSE.
WELL, IT'S NOT LIKE I CARED ANY-WAY.
IRK
AMANDA!
WHAT ARE YOU TALKING ALL BIG FOR!?
NOT LIKE YOU GUYS ARE THAT MUCH STRONGER!
HUH?
SAY WHAT? WHADDAYA MEAN?
ALL CONSTANZE DOES IS MESS AROUND WITH MACHINES...
...AND JASMINKA JUST EATS ALL THE TIME!
WANT SOME?
THANKS!

BUT THEY'RE BOTH BETTER AT MAGIC THAN YOU.

URK...

MY, MY. THE DROP-OUTS AND THE DELIN-QUENTS TOGETH-ER.

WHAT DO THEY CALL THIS AGAIN?

EYE GUNK MAKING FUN OF SNOT?

OH, EWWW! HOW VULGAR.

HEE HEE! くす

HEE HEE! くす

IN THAT CASE—

MAY ALL OF YOU ...

CLICK
CLICK

... PLAY FAIR!

WILL THEY BE ALL RIGHT?

DIANA!
!

WHAT YOU SAID BEFORE... IF I WIN...

...TAKE IT BACK.
...

DO AS YOU LIKE.
I MEAN IT!
FWEEET

TOSS
OKAY!
BOUNCE
HERE IT COMES!
HUP!
OKAY!
DIANA!
TMP
WHEW!
SHFF
...

WALL.
SPAKK
!
HUH?
BUT I DIDN'T TOUCH IT...
?
HUH. NOW THAT'S AN IDEA.
...
TMP
WAS THAT ...!?

MAGIC !?
EXCUSE ME!? DID YOU JUST USE MAGIC !?
NO FAIR!
WHAT'S WRONG WITH A WITCH USING MAGIC?
ARE YOU DUMB OR SOMETHING?
THAT BRAZEN... HOW DARE SHE!?
REF! THAT WAS A FOUL!
FUGO?
?
THIS GUY'S USE-LESS!!

IF THAT'S WHAT THEY WANT TO DO, LET THEM.
SHF
HOW-EVER—!

HAVE YOU FORGOTTEN ABOUT YOUR TEAMMATES?
!
HUH!?

TUMP
HEH HEH HEH!
SQUEAL SQUEAL
NO PROBLEMS HERE, I SEE. GOOD.
MM-HM, MM-HM.
O WIND!
HM?

TWIST AND WIND!!

VREEN

AKKO!

GHK ...!

WHUD

RECEIVE WITH MAGIC!

I HAVEN'T LEARNED HOW TO DO THAT YET!!

ス
DODGE
ッ...
!?
10 01
17 01
?
23 01
AWWW! FOR CRYIN' OUT LOUD!!
UM, EXCUSE ME!
FRET
オロ
FRET
オロ
MAGIC ISN'T ...

AMANDA!
I'M DONE! THIS IS STUPID!
BUT!
WHO'D WASTE THEIR TIME ON STUFF LIKE THIS?
SHF
BESIDES...
WHIZ
AMANDA!!
WHOOSH
—!
SPAKK

SKIIID

OW, OW, OW!

PEH! PTOOEY!

HEY!

WHY SO DESPERATE?

IT'S JUST A GAME.

SHE...

SHE MADE FUN OF CHARIOT.

HUH?

CHARIOT TAUGHT ME MAGIC IS SOMETHING MAGNIFICENT.

SHE SAID SHE CAN'T CONDONE CHARIOT'S MAGIC, AND THAT'S...

THAT'S JUST WRONG!

I'M GONNA MAKE HER TAKE IT BACK NO MATTER WHAT!

...FOR AFTER YOU WIN!

WHIZZ

LUNGE

AKKO!

NGH!
FWISH
!?
TMP
THEN THAT WAS...
KASHUNK
STANBOT!?

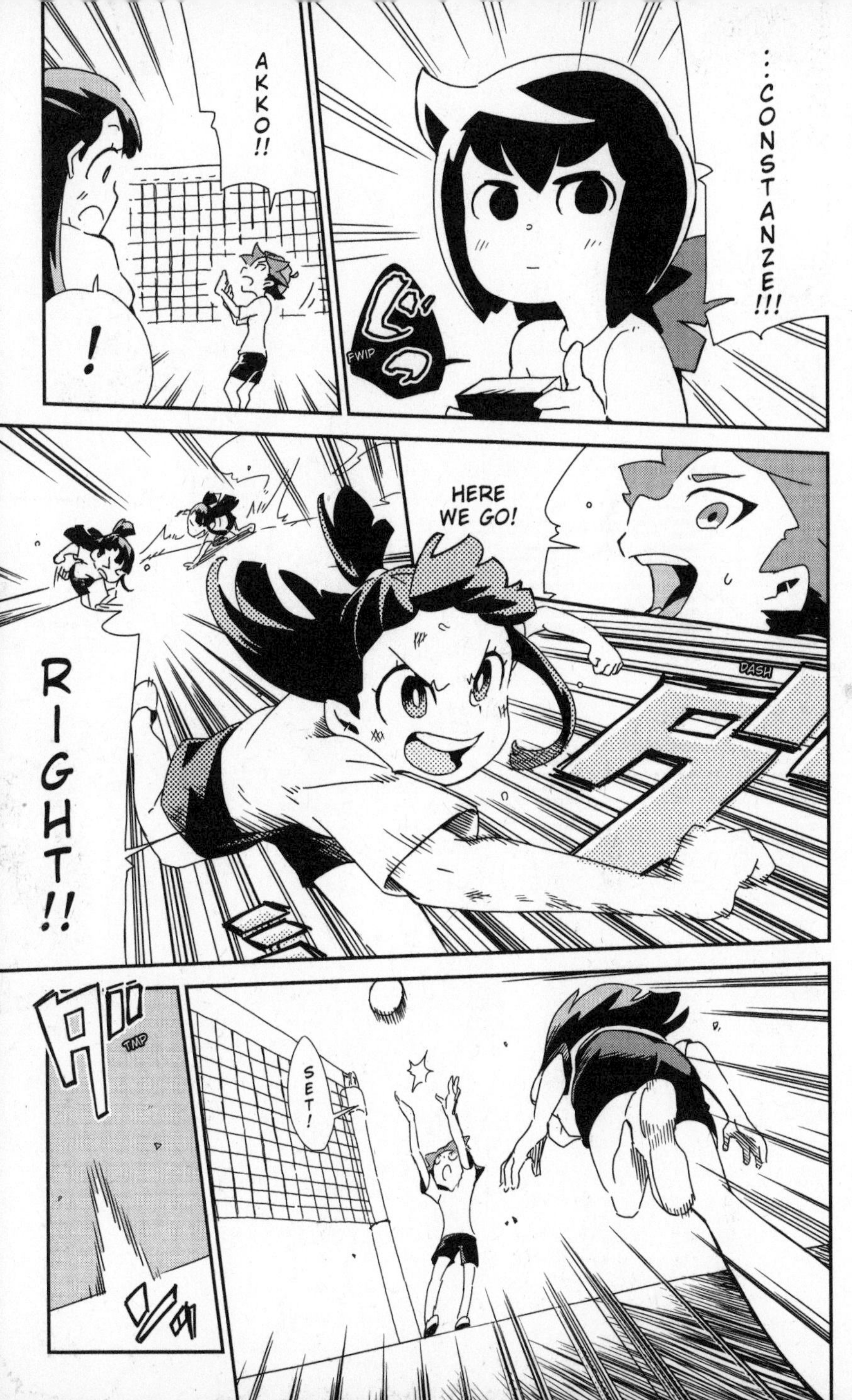
...CONSTANZE!!!
FWIP
AKKO!!
!
HERE WE GO!
DASH
RIGHT!!
SET!
TMP

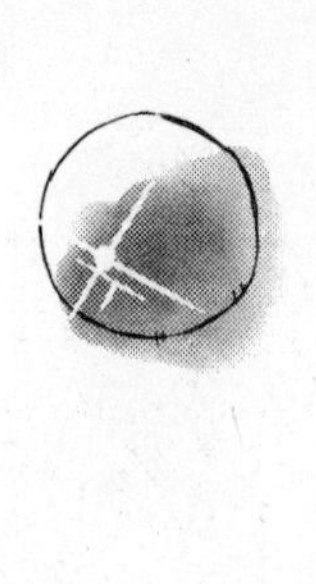

UUUUU!

25 02

WE LOOOO-OOOST!

LIKE WE COULD ACTUALLY WIN. ARE YOU STUPID?

GUSH

GUSH

GUSH

GUSH

GUSH

MEANIE!

BWOOSH

IT WAS PRETTY FUN, THOUGH.

HUP...

YOU'VE GOT GUTS...

...AKKO.

JUST GUTS, THOUGH.
HEY!
WHAT'S THAT S'POSED TO MEAN !?

GOODNESS!

HELLO! GIRLS!
DON'T BE LATE FOR YOUR NEXT CLASSES!

I SWEAR. THANKS TO AKKO, WE'RE A TOTAL MESS.

THE GIRL'S DEFEC-TIVE.
SHE JUST DOESN'T KNOW WHEN TO GIVE UP. RIGHT, DIANA?
YES.

HOWEVER...
THAT'S JUST WRONG!
I'M GONNA MAKE HER TAKE IT BACK NO MATTER WHAT!

I'M SORRY.

DID YOU SAY SOMETHING, DIANA?

IT WAS NOTHING.

Little Witch Academia

Little Witch Academia

Chapter 4 BROOM FLIGHT SHOW!!

AND DOWN WE... GO!
WHUD

WHEW! I'M BEEEAT!
TNK
TNK
WHY'D THEY MAKE US BRING THE SHOOTING STAR BACK ANYWAY?
I HEARD IT WAS THE PENALTY FOR STEALING IT.
AKKO, YOU DIDN'T!
HUH!?

NO WAY! IT'S A FALSE CHARGE!
LOOM
GEEZ... IT'S GOOD IT'S BACK AT LEAST, BUT...
...GIMME A BREAK, WOULD YA?

LOOK, IT WASN'T ME! BESIDES, IF WE'RE GONNA "RETURN" IT...

SPLOOSH

TAP

PWAH!

UH, YEAH...SURE...

...IT SHOULD BE TO ITS OWNER!!

WHAT IS IT, AKKO?

NOT EVEN POSSIBLE! THE OWNER'S MISSING...

DING

WHOOPS. CUSTOMER.

I BET SHE'S GOT ANOTHER LOUSY IDEA.

IT CAN'T BE DONE, AKKO.

THE SHOOTING STAR...

...DOESN'T HAVE A SPIRIT LIVING IN IT.

BESIDES, TOOLS HAVE TO BE AT LEAST A HUNDRED YEARS OLD TO ACQUIRE A SPIRIT.

B-BUT! BUT!

My First Broom Ride

THE TEXTBOOK I GOT FROM PROFESSOR URSULA SAID, "FORM A TRUSTING RELATIONSHIP WITH YOUR BROOM."

DOESN'T THAT MEAN THE BROOM HAS A MIND OF ITS OWN?

PFFT!

YOU'RE THE ONLY ONE WHO'D BUY THAT, AKKO.
HAW! HAW! HAW!
IT'S JUST WRITTEN SIMPLY, FOR LITTLE KIDS!
AKKO, THAT'S NOT QUITE...
YOU TWO ARE SO MEAN!
I'M SERIOUS ABOUT THIS!
FINE! I'LL LOOK ON MY OWN!
DASH
AKKO!
THAT WASN'T NICE OF US, WAS IT...?
I BET IT'LL BE FINE.
......

WHAT, YOU'RE THE LIAR-WITCH!?
SHE SAYS TOOLS CAN TALK.
THE SPIRITS...
SPIRITS? HAT STUFF DOESN'T EXIST!
LIIIAR.
LIIIAR!!
...
...DO EXIST...

IF YOU'VE SEEN
THIS BROOM,
CONTACT ME!!
by AKKO KAGARI
OH NO...
SHE'S REALLY INTO THIS...
STU-PIDLY INTO IT.
WHAT'S THE POINT OF DOING THIS AT SCHOOL ...?

A-ANYWAY, WE HAVE TO STOP HER.
BEFORE A TEACHER CATCHES HER!
TOO LATE.
YOU AGAIN, MISS KAGARI!?
AUGH!!
AND IT'S PROFESSOR FINNELAN TOO...!

WHAT'S GOING ON...?
I BET AKKO BLEW IT AGAIN.
"SEEKING OWNER OF BROOM."
WHAT!? THAT'S HILARIOUS!
...

...SUCY, LISTEN...
?
WHEN I WAS LITTLE, THE NEIGHBORHOOD KIDS PICKED ON ME.

THEY SAID, "WITCHES ARE LIARS," AND "SPIRITS DON'T EXIST."
MAYBE THAT'S WHY...

...I UNDER-STAND HOW AKKO FEELS ...
... JUST A LITTLE.

!
TMP

GOOD GRIEF...

SHE COULD'VE LET ME KEEP A FEW UP. OLD STICK-IN-THE-MUD!
HMPH!!
AKKO! I HAVE AN IDEA...
AN IDEA?
YOU MEAN YOU'LL HELP!?
IS THAT OKAY?
YES! ABSOLUTELY!!

I'LL PASS.
HUH!?
GLIDE
HEY! SU, WAIT!!
STINGY!! HEART-LESS!!
AND YOU'RE DROPPING THOSE!

HMPH! SEE IF I ASK HER AGAIN!
SHE'S PROB-ABLY BUSY...

PEEK
PEEK
TUP
TUP
LOTTE, THAT'S AMAZ-ING!
PEEK
SO THOSE DO EXIST...

...THE SHOOTING STAR'S SPIRIT ISN'T—
CLUNK
CLUNK
...I SEE ...
......
SO I WAS JUST IMAGINING...
!
AKKO!
WHIP
I'LL TRY ONE MORE TIME!

I MIGHT HAVE MADE A MISTAKE.
SNIFFLE
うるるる
LOTTE...
TMP
OKAY! IN THAT CASE, I'LL GO ASK AROUND TOWN!
YOU COME HELP TOO, MISTER!
HUH!?
HEY, I HAVE TO WATCH THE SHOP—
GRANDMA, YOU'RE SINGING AGAIN.
HM?
OH, YES.
BUT THOSE TOOLS DON'T HAVE SPIRITS IN THEM YET.
WELL, THAT'S TRUE.
?
BUT, LOTTE, THERE'S NO TOOL THAT DOESN'T HAVE A SPIRIT IN IT.

LISTEN, LOTTE.
TOOL SPIRITS ARE—

TINKLE
HUH? JUST YOU, LOTTE?
!
SUCY!? WHY...?

I WAS DOING SOME RESEARCH AT THE LIBRARY, AND I **STUMBLED** ONTO...
...AN ARTICLE ON THE SHOOTING STAR.
I FIGURED I'D TEASE AKKO WITH IT.
KEH! HEH! HEH!
HONESTLY, SUCY...
TINKLE
WAAAH... NOBODY KNEW A THING, LOTTEEEE!

HUNH!?
SUCY FOUND AN ARTICLE ON THE SHOOTING STAR!
SU!? WHY ARE YOU HERE!?
"NEVER MIND"!?
NEVER MIND THAT! LET'S READ THIS, AKKO!
WHAT WAS THAT!!?
IT LOOKS LIKE ALL THAT WASTED WORK MADE YOU A LITTLE SMARTER.
"A METEOR FALLS—
"THE SPEED STAR OF THE WITCH WORLD"!

THIS WAS PUBLISHED ON...
NOVEMBER 1, 1985
"AFTER FALLING FROM HER PARTNER, THE SHOOTING STAR, SHE MADE A MIRACULOUS RECOVERY AND LAUNCHED THE 'ULTRA-EXPRESS WITCH'S DELIVERY SERVICE,' ACHIEVING A GUINNESS RECORD FOR HIGHEST TOTAL NUMBER OF DELIVERIES.
"SHE STAYED ACTIVE, CONTINUING TO WORK UNTIL LATE IN LIFE, BUT FINALLY PASSED ON."

I'M SORRY, SHOOTING STAR.

AKKO...

IT LOOKS LIKE I WON'T BE ABLE TO RETURN YOU TO YOUR OWNER.

THERE'S NOT MUCH MORE WE CAN DO.
TNK
TNK
I KNOW...
BONK
TNK
TNK
TNK
TNK
THUD
HUH!?
HUH!? WHA—!? WHY DID IT JUST FALL OVER LIKE THAT!?
TWIRL
ZOOM

!?
HEBWAGH!?
KERWHAM
DUMMY! THE SPELL'S GONE OUT OF CONTROL!
I-IS THE SHOOTING STAR ANGRY!?
CRASH
YAAA-AAAGH! IT'S COMING THIS WAY!
WHIZ
CLANK

WHOOOSH
WHIZZ
IT FLEW OFF...
DOESN'T THAT MEAN IT WAS JUST A TOOL?
OOOO
THAT CAN'T BE...
OOOO
... STILL...

AUGH!
ZIP
SCREECH
WHAT'S WITH THIS, UH... BROOM!?
BONK
CRASH
WHUD
HUH? DON'T TELL ME...
BONK
CLANG
THE SHOOTING STAR? WHY......?
SNAP
KABOOM

IT CAME BACK!!?

WHIZZ
FLAP

HM?

WHERE ARE WE?

ON THE SHOOTING STAR, IT LOOKS LIKE.

DOWN ...?

OH.

LISTEN, LOTTE.

SPIRITS DON'T MOVE INTO ANYTHING.

THEY DON'T?
NO, THEY DON'T. SPIRITS...

...ARE BORN!

IT DIIID, HUH?
THE SHOOTING STAR'S SPIRIT...

IT SAID, "I'M LEAVING ON A JOURNEY TO FIND A SUITABLE MASTER" AND FLEW OFF SOMEWHERE?
I SEE. WOW. HOW 'BOUT THAT.

...REALLY?
YES, REALLY!
YOU'RE SURE YOU'RE NOT JUST...
...PLANNING TO MAKE OFF WITH IT AGAI—
IRK

ZOOM

IT'S TRUE! I SPOKE WITH THE SHOOTING STAR!

BESIDES, AKKO HAS NO INTENTION OF STEALING IT!

!

R-RIGHT.

...IS ALL ON YOU.

HUH?

Little Witch Academia

Little Witch Academia

Chapter 5

THE HISTORY OF WITCHES BEGAN IN THE MEGALITHIC CIVILIZATION AND DECLINED ALONG WITH IT.

HOWEVER, NINE WITCHES APPEARED. THEIR POWER HALTED THE DECAY...

...AND THE WITCHES RETOOK THEIR STRENGTH...

THE NINE WITCHES...
HM?
TWITCH
IF I LOOK INTO THEM, I MAY FIND A WAY TO...
THE GROUP THAT RESTORED THE WITCHES AFTER THEIR DECLINE, THEN FOUNDED LUNA NOVA.
CLINK
THE AROMA OF THIS TEA... WHAT IS IT?
PLUM SEAWEED TEA. WHAT ABOUT IT?
PEEK
!?

Chapter 5 PANIC MUSHROOM PARTY

YOU!
CLATTER
WHAT ARE YOU DOING IN MY ROOM ...?
OH, BE QUIET.
SULK
AND ...
...WHAT IS GOING ON...
...WITH THOSE CLOTHES ?
URK!
W-WELL, MY ALLOWANCE WAS CUT— I MEAN, IT HASN'T COME THIS MONTH...
...SO I HAD TO HAVE THE OFFICE GOBLIN SET ME UP WITH A PART-TIME JOB.
THUMP
SO YOUR GRADES WERE SO DISMAL, THEY REVOKED YOUR ALLOWANCE.
NGH ...!

AT ANY RATE! IT WOULD BE A NUISANCE TO HAVE YOU IN CHARGE OF THIS ROOM.
I'LL SPEAK TO THE CLERK ABOUT IT FOR YOU, SO...

...GET OUT.

YOU CAN'T DO THAT TO ME!!
!?
LOOM

THE THING IS...

SAY WHAT!?
QUIET! I'M MIXING MEDICINE OVER HERE!
B-BUT, I MEAN, MY ALLOWANCE ...

NOW, EVEN IF I GO TO TOWN, I WON'T BE ABLE TO DO ANYTHING—!
GLOOM
OH, IT'S NOT THAT BAD...
RIDICU-LOUS.

COME TO THINK OF IT, I'VE NEVER SEEN YOU GET AN ALLOWANCE, SUCY.
AS A RULE, I'M LEFT TO MY OWN DEVICES.
POOF

I'M FROM A BIG FAMILY, YOU SEE.
SO! SO!
YOU GET TO HAVE LOTS OF BIRTHDAY PARTIES THAT WAY, RIGHT!?
THAT'S WHAT MATTERS TO YOU, AKKO?
HUH!
THAT'S KINDA SUR-PRISING.
BEAM
BIRTHDAYS!
THOSE SPECIAL DAYS WHEN YOU GET TO BE THE STAR!
EVEN IF YOU'RE A BIT PLAYER, YOU STILL GET...
...TO CHOW DOWN...
TUG
OF COURSE WE DON'T DO STUFF LIKE THAT.
HUH!?
BIRTHDAYS ARE POINTLESS.
THAT'S NOT TRUE! WHAT A WASTE!
HUH?
A WASTE?

Let's Party
I KNOW! I'LL CELEBRATE WITH YOU!!
PUMP
NO. I'M GOOD.
LOOK FORWARD TO IT!!
DASH
WAVE
WAVE
LISTEN WHEN I TELL YOU STUFF.
......
AND SO, IN ORDER TO CELEBRATE, I NEED MONEY.
LIFE MUST BE DIFFICULT FOR THOSE OTHER GIRLS AS WELL...
I STILL CAN'T LEAVE THIS ROOM IN YOUR CARE.
WHY NOT !!?

IN THAT CASE, I JUST HAD A GREAT IDEA!

KACHAK

A-AKKO !?

DASH

JOLT

EEP!

HUH!? WHY ARE YOU—

HON-ESTLY...

SIGH

MY. THIS ISN'T BAD.

I'VE CALLED YOU HERE FOR A REASON.

I WANT YOU TO HELP ME...

...GET A SURPRISE PRESENT FOR SUCY'S BIRTHDAY.

'SCUSE ME?

A SURPRISE PRESENT FOR SUCY?

C'MON! LET'S JUST DO IT! I WANNA DO IT FOR HER!

HEH!
SO DO IT. ON YOUR OWN.

IRK

!
MUTTER
COME TO THINK OF IT, I WAS ACCUSED—FALSELY—OF STEALING THE SHOOTING STAR THE OTHER DAY.

HUH! THAT'S ROUGH. BUT WHY BRING IT UP NOW?
DON'T TELL ME YOU SUSPECT YOUR FRIENDS?
CREAK
NOOOO, NOT AT ALL. I'D NEVER SUSPECT A FRIEND...
......!
STAAAARE
DURING THE BROOM RACE, YOU SAID SOMETHING THAT'S BEEN ON MY MIND, BUT I DON'T SUSPECT YOU. AFTER ALL, WE'RE FRIENDS.

Y-YEAH, WE SURE ARE! WE'RE DEFINITELY FRIENDS. WELL, I GUESS IT'S GOTTA BE DONE. I'LL HELP YOU OUT.
CLATTER
THAT'S MY AMANDA!
CONSEY AND JASMINKA, YOU'RE IN TOO?
NOD
DOINK
SO, DO YOU HAVE ANY IDEAS FOR THIS PRESENT?
OF COURSE!
WE'RE GOING HUNTING FOR POISONOUS MUSHROOMS!
HUH?

OH.

I HAVEN'T EXPERIMENTED WITH AKKO TODAY.

!!

SPROING

Y-YOU KNOW, YOU COULD TAKE A BREAK FROM EXPERIMENTING NOW AND THEN.
YOU'RE RIGHT. I SHOULD CHANGE MY TEST SUBJECTS NOW AND THEN.
TEST SUB-JECTS !!?
C-C-CALM DOWN, SUCY!!
PANIC
PANIC
INCH
INCH
IF YOU USE ME, I WON'T BE ABLE TO GO TO CLASS TOMORROW.
IT'S FINE. I WON'T USE ANY-THING THAT POTENT.
BADUM
SQUIKK
THERE'S NOTHING FINE ABOUT... AH!
A-A-ALL RIGHT! ALL RIGHT! I'LL TALK!
I'LL TALK, OKAY !? AKKO'S GOING TO—

I KNEW IT...

THE GIRL'S A MEDDLER, AS USUAL.

UU... UH-HUH...

HFFFF!

SQUEAK

IT'S NOT A SURPRISE IF YOU ANNOUNCE IT FIRST ANYWAY.

I'M SORRY, AKKO. I'M NOT AS STURDY AS YOU ARE...

TALKED

AS A RESULT, I HAVE THREE OLDER BROTHERS, FOUR OLDER SISTERS, FIVE YOUNGER BROTHERS, AND TWO LITTLE SISTERS, AND THEN THERE'S RAMZA'S APPRENTICES, A FEW RELATIVES, ETCETERA...
THAT'S A LOT!!
WITH ALL THOSE PEOPLE, SOMEBODY'S ALWAYS CELEBRATING SOMEBODY ELSE'S BIRTHDAY.
THAT SOUNDS LIKE FUN.
IT'S JUST ANNOY-ING.

SHUF
ALL RIGHT. I'LL GO FIND AKKO.
OH. RIGHT...
SAY, RAMZA? IS THERE ANY POINT IN CELEBRATING BIRTHDAYS?

I HAD THREE OF THEM THIS MONTH.
THEN YOU LUCKED OUT.
I GUESS ...
THERE'S NO POINT IN BIRTHDAYS.
HUH?

THERE'S NO POINT, BUT THERE ARE FEELINGS.
THEY ALL JUST WANT TO CELEBRATE THE FACT THAT YOU WERE BORN INTO THIS WORLD.

......

OH... WAIT, SUCY!
AKKO'S REALLY EAGER TO MAKE YOU HAPPY. YOU COULD GO ALONG WITH IT...
HAS ANYTHING GOOD EVER HAPPENED WHEN AKKO'S REALLY EAGER?
W-WELL, UM...

THOOM
THOOM
THOOM
THOOM
THOOM

WHAT THE HECK ARE THOSE !?

HEY, AKKO!
AREN'T THEY CHASING US TO GET THAT MUSHROOM BACK!?
THOOM
THOOM
THOOM
THOOM
WHAT!!?
HUH!? BUT...
LET'S JUST GIVE IT TO 'EM ALREADY.
SHE AIN'T GONNA BE HAPPY WITH IT ANY-WAY.
THAT'S NOT TRUE!

THIS IS ALL FOR YOUR SELF-SATISFACTION! YOU CAN'T CELEBRATE LIKE THAT!

HUH!? THAT'S NOT WHAT I'M AFTER!

AND ANYWAY, THAT'S NO REASON...

...NOT TO CELEBRATE HER BIRTHDAY!

—!

AH!

CREEP
CREEP
CREEP
WAAAAAAH!
GHK!
CREEP
CREEP
ENOUGH! GIMME THAT THING! I'LL GIVE IT BACK!
NO, WAIT! THERE MUST BE ANOTHER WAY—
GRAB
DON'T YOU CARE WHAT HAPPENS TO CONSEY!!?
I DIDN'T SAY THAT!
SHOVE
!
!

NO...
IRK
... FIGHT-ING!

HMPH!
TCH!
AKKO.
PLEASE!
!

......
SQUEEZE
'KAY!

RAAAAAAAA
AAAAAAAGH!

LET CONSTANZE...
...GOOOOOOOOOOOOOO!!!
WHOOSH
FLING
THOOM
THOOM
THOOM
THOOM

SUCY! OVER THERE!
HM?
THEY'RE ALL...
UUU...
UHNN...
UGH.
...ASLEEP?

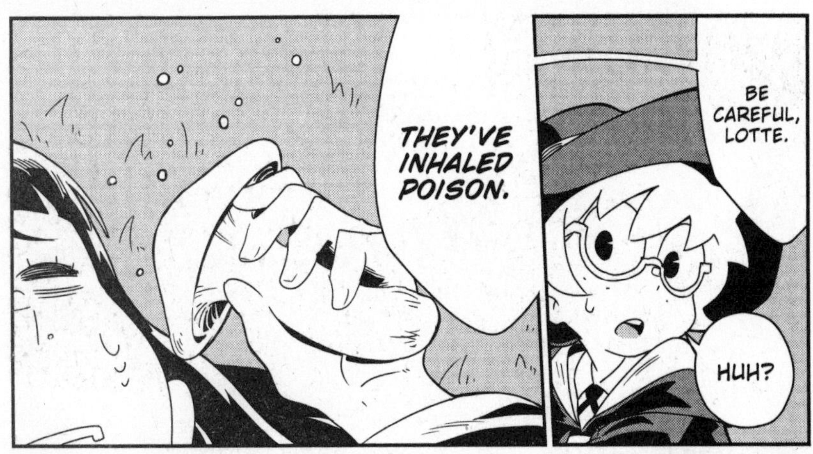

WILL THEY BE OKAY?
SQUIK
THE TOXIN IN THESE MUSHROOMS WON'T KILL YOU.
ALL IT DOES IS GIVE YOU NIGHTMARES. I GAVE THEM THE ANTIDOTE, SO THEY'LL WAKE UP SOON.

UNGH... I'M SORRY, SU...
UGH...
YOUR PRESENT WILL HAVE TO WAIT...
HN?!
BLINK
AKKO!

SORRY ...

DROOP

!

SUCY! HERE! YOUR PRESE—

FOR YOUR BIRTH-DAY —!

SNATCH

I COLLECTED THAT PIDDLING ONE AGES AGO.

FLING

HUH!?

...I'LL ACCEPT THE FEELINGS BEHIND IT.

BUT...
"THAT PIDDLING ONE"...

SUCY!!
BEAAM
H-HEY!

WHAT IS THAT THING?
HMM?

A D—
WHOOSH
DRAGON!?

TO THINK THEY'D TAKE...

...THE SOR-CERER'S STONE—!!

LITTLE WITCH ACADEMIA ① ...... THE END

Little Witch Academia

Character Introductions
ATSUKO KAGARI
A cheerful, optimistic girl from Japan who wants to become a witch.
OHHH...
HUH!?
HEE HEE HEE!

Character Design
SUCY MANBAVARAN
Akko's roommate. She's sarcastic and does things her way. Poison fiend.
?
LOTTE JANSSON
Akko's roommate. A kind, sincere girl. She's able to use songs to summon spirits.
HEH -HEH HEH!
AH HA HA!

AFTERWORD
HELLO THERE. I'M SATO, WHO, ALTHOUGH TERRIBLY UNWORTHY, HAS BEEN GRANTED THE HONOR OF DRAWING THE MANGA VERSION OF LITTLE WITCH ACADEMIA.
SHOW SOME RESPECT.
GNAW
GNAW
YOUR WORDS AND YOUR ATTITUDE DON'T MATCH.

IN THIS SERIES, I PLAN TO FOLLOW THE ANIME WHILE WORKING IN ORIGINAL EPISODES.
ANNABEL-CHAN, AUTHOR OF LOTTE'S BELOVED NIGHT FALL
night fall
FLINCH FLINCH
FOR A WIMP...
...YOU'RE SURPRISINGLY IMPUDENT, AREN'T YOU?
WELL, I WANTED BOTH FANS OF THE ANIME AND FIRST-TIMERS TO ENJOY IT!
KNOW YOUR PLACE.
SAYS THE ONE ALWAYS GETTING TRASHED ONLINE!
WHAT DID YOU SAY!?

Thank you for reading!
STEAM
FINALLY, THANK YOU VERY MUCH FOR PICKING UP THIS BOOK.
Staff
MANGA: SATO
COLORIST: UKU-SAN
EDITOR: OZAKI-SAN
DESIGN: KUBO-SAN
See you Again!

Little Witch Academia

Little Witch Academia

Original Story: TRIGGER / YOH YOSHINARI
Art: KEISUKE SATO

Translation: TAYLOR ENGEL ✦ Lettering: TAKESHI KAMURA

JY
1290 Avenue of the Americas
New York, NY 10104

Visit us at yenpress.com ✦ facebook.com/yenpress ✦ twitter.com/yenpress ✦ yenpress.tumblr.com ✦ instagram.com/yenpress

First JY Edition: June 2018

JY is an imprint of Yen Press, LLC.
The JY name and logo are trademarks of Yen Press, LLC.

The publisher is not responsible for websites (or their content) that are not owned by the publisher.

Library of Congress Control Number: 2018935620

ISBNs: 978-1-9753-2745-3 (paperback)
978-1-9753-8246-9 (ebook)

10 9 8 7 6 5 4 3

WOR

Printed in the United States of America